MAGIC FACES

INTRODUCING . . .

Austin

Ozzy

Magic Face
Painting Kit

Alanna

Aunty
Kessie

With special thanks to Stella Botchway

For Sam, Little Sarah, the Botchways and Sue – E.M.

For everyone who's been there since the beginning – A.T.

Magic Faces: Heroes of the Pirate Ship is a uclanpublishing book

First published in Great Britain in 2023 by
uclanpublishing
University of Central Lancashire
Preston, PR1 2HE, UK

Text copyright © Storymix Limited, 2023
Illustrations copyright © Abeeha Tariq, 2023
Series created by Storymix Limited
Edited by Clare Whitson

978-1-915235-06-0

3 5 7 9 10 8 6 4 2

A CIP catalogue record for this book is available from the British Library.

Printed and bound in Great Britain by Page Bros Group.

ESI
MERLEH

MAGIC FACES

HEROES of the PIRATE SHIP

Illustrated by
ABEEHA TARIQ

uclanpublishing

CHAPTER ONE

"Hey, what are you two going to make your aunty for dinner? I'm getting hungry with all this painting!" Aunty Kessie splattered some more green paint onto a big piece of paper rolled out on a large wooden table.

Austin and his twin sister, Alanna, looked up from their game of pirate snap.

"We're kids, Aunty. We can't cook!" Austin said.

"Hmm." Aunty Kessie looked disappointed. "Maybe Ozzy can cook us up some jollof rice?"

Ozzy the sausage dog was nestled in his basket in the corner of the art studio. He lifted his ears and raised his little eyebrows in surprise.

"Stop messing about, Aunty Kessie," Austin said.

"And anyway, Ozzy says he's too busy." Alanna grinned.

Aunty Kessie smiled back, flashing her big round dimples. "Ah well, I guess it's my turn to cook then!" She cocked her head to one side. "Why don't you two twin peas paint a picture while I'm gone?"

"OK! I know just what to paint." Alanna grabbed a paintbrush and went straight for the orange. "I'm going to do a sunset."

Austin picked up a brush and looked down at his blank piece of paper.

Aunty Kessie tapped him on the nose. "What will you draw, Austin?"

"I don't know."

"You'll come up with something – just go with what's in your heart."

Aunty went to the kitchen, and Austin watched Alanna flicking orange paint onto the paper in big, fat dollops. Austin sighed. His twin always knew exactly what she wanted.

Austin put his paintbrush down and looked around for something else to do. Aunty's art studio was his favourite room in the house because it was crammed with things to play with. There were stickers and sequins, colouring pencils, crayons, pastels and pens. A flash of silver on a nearby shelf caught Austin's eye. A metal box lay half hidden between sketchpads, paint pots and lumps of clay wrapped in cling film. Austin had never noticed this box before. He stood on his tip-toes and reached up high.

"Gotcha!"

He pulled hard. The box came down, but so did a jar of beads and tubes of rolled-up paper. Austin yelped as he dodged out of the way, holding the box in his arms.

Alanna came to his side. "What are you up to?"

Austin held up the battered metal box in answer. The faded label on it said '*Magic Faces!*'

"Cool," Alanna said. "Erm, what is it?"

Ozzy bounded over and jumped up, pushing at the tin with his nose.

"Careful, Ozzy!" said Austin. "You'll make me drop it." He lifted the little clasp, and the lid sprung open to reveal some face paints and a paintbrush . . . that was moving!

The twins watched in amazement as the wooden paintbrush with its short fat tip

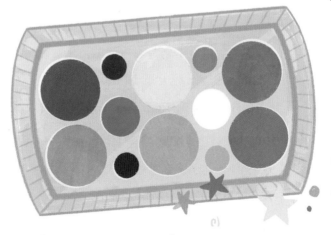

floated up into the air in a burst of sparkles. The brush did a little dance, as if pleased to be released from its dusty tin.

"Whoa!" Austin breathed.

"Magic paintbrushes aren't real, are they Austin?" whispered Alanna, clutching his arm.

The brush darted forward and tickled Alanna on the nose, then tickled Austin.

"*Aaichoo!*" Austin sneezed.

"It definitely *feels* real!" he said.

The paintbrush twirled in a circle again. Showers of silver sparks flew out from the tip, leaving pretty swirls in the air.

"Look! It's writing!" cried Alanna.

The paintbrush twirled and quivered and looped, this time leaving words on the lid of the tin in bold writing:

PIRATE SHIP OR ROBOT WORLD:

Which one will you choose?
In each a race to find the prize . . .
Will you win or lose?

"Erm . . . pirate ship or robot world? I can't pick," Austin said.

The paintbrush bobbed up and down, waiting.

"Austin, we love pirates – let's go for that!" said Alanna.

"Erm . . . OK. Can we have pirates please?" Austin asked, nervously.

The paintbrush whipped around and dipped its brush into a square of red paint. It flew to Austin's face, dancing over his cheeks and forehead.

"It tickles!" he said, trying not to laugh.

"Keep still, Austin," Alanna said. "It's painting something on you."

Austin squeezed his eyes shut and his fists tight to stop himself from moving. The bristles were tingly and every time it touched his face, he could feel magic dancing across his skin.

The brush finished its work and Alanna gasped.

"You look awesome," Alanna said.

Without wasting any time, the paintbrush painted a blue watch on Austin's wrist with a blank, yellow face and then hopped over to

Alanna. In a flurry of colour, it started to paint her face as well.

Austin couldn't stop smiling as he watched the paintbrush whizz over his sister's cheeks.

The end of the brush dipped into the purple and drew a bandana across Alanna's forehead. The brush finished with an anchor shaped tattoo on her cheek. She looked amazing!

Austin grabbed the lid of an old biscuit tin holding scraps of collage paper. Alanna ran to his side and he flipped the lid over to look at the shiny surface.

"Wow!"

A red bandana stretched across Austin's forehead, the knotted ends hanging down

past his ear. He had two wild, dark eyebrows and stubble covered his chin.

"Pirates." Alanna whooped. "We look just like pirates!"

CHAPTER TWO

The paintbrush was busy wiping away the rhyme on its lid, and in its place painted a picture of a bright yellow box.

"That's got to be the prize the rhyme spoke about," said Alanna. "It looks like a treasure chest."

"That makes sense," Austin replied. "All pirates hunt for treasure!"

Austin looked around the messy studio.

"It'll take us a whole day to find it in here."

Alanna started by opening one of the desk drawers. It was full of felt tip pens, but no chest.

Suddenly, the door to the back garden burst open with a bang. It made Austin jump. He turned, but instead of seeing the garden through the doors, all he could see was thick grey mist. *That's strange . . .*

"Can you smell that?" asked Alanna.

Austin took a deep sniff. "Aunty must be cooking fish soup. I hope she doesn't burn it this time!"

"It was only a little burnt," said Alanna. "You could eat *most* of it . . . but I don't think it's her cooking."

She ran to the garden door, sticking her head outside. "Can you hear that?"

Austin nodded, sure that he could hear singing coming from the mist swirling outside. And then the sound of rolling waves and seagulls! *This is getting weird*, he thought. *We don't live by the sea.*

Before Austin could say anything, Alanna ran out of the back door and disappeared into the mist.

"Alanna! Come back!"

Austin ran after Alanna, his heart pounding. But instead of running out onto Aunty Kessie's concrete patio, the ground under his feet was slippery and wooden! He held his arms out like an aeroplane for balance and called again for his sister.

Then as quickly as it had arrived, the mist around Austin disappeared and a spray of water hit him square in the face. Wiping the salt water from his eyes and mouth he looked around in amazement. He was standing on the deck of a busy pirate ship!

"This is STRAMAZING," Alanna said, running over to Austin. "That's strange and amazing all at the same time by the way."

"Jumpin' Joe and Climbin' Cleo," a pirate said, walking over to them. "Ye both looks good and nimble. Ye can be on lookout."

Alanna grabbed Austin's arm and squeezed it tight in excitement. "She thinks we're pirates!"

"And we have pirate names!" said Austin, bouncing on the spot.

"To go with our pirate clothes!" added Alanna. She strutted up and down the deck showing off the tattered top and shorts, which had magically replaced her normal clothes.

"To the crow's nest, the pair o' ye!" said the pirate, flinging them a telescope. "If anyone asks, tell 'em Sour Sal sent you."

Something fluffy brushed against Austin's leg. He looked down to see Ozzy huddled up next to him.

Alanna bent down to pick him up. "Nice to see you boy. What's wrong?"

Ozzy whined.

"Don't you want to go up the rigging?" she asked.

Ozzy tipped his head back to look up at the crow's nest at the top of the pole and gave another little whine.

"Don't worry Ozzy, you don't have to go up," said Austin. He saw an empty barrel nearby and settled Ozzy into it. "We'll be back soon."

Austin and Alanna began to climb up the rigging. The rope swayed

in the wind and they had to cling on really tightly.

Up in the crow's nest, the wind whistled around them. The sea stretched in every direction, blue and twinkling. The ship's pirate's flag flapped with a crack and a pop.

Alanna put the telescope to her eye. "It's all fuzzy," she said.

"That's because it's the wrong way round," Austin said, taking it from her and turning it the right way. "Can you see the treasure chest anywhere?"

"I can't see anything but sea," she replied.

"Let me look," Austin said, waving his arms in front of the telescope to get Alanna's attention. As he did, he noticed the

watch the paintbrush had painted onto his wrist. A tiny thin wedge was shaded blue.

"Maybe when the whole watch face is blue, our time is up?" Alanna said, lowering the telescope.

"What do you think happens if we still haven't found the treasure chest when that happens??" asked Austin.

Alanna shrugged her shoulders.

"Well, it looks like we don't have long to find out!" said Austin, studying the watch again.

Alanna put the telescope back to her eye. "A boat!" she cried out, handing the telescope to Austin.

Two people were rowing a small boat towards the ship. They were wearing pirate hats and pulling and pushing the oars with all their might. They were still quite far away, but getting closer with each stroke.

"Approaching pirates, port side!" yelled Alanna.

The Big Book of Pirate Facts was one of Alanna and Austin's favourite books. They knew all about using port for the left side of the ship and starboard for the right!

Alanna sighed. "I don't think anyone heard me. Come on, we've got to find the captain and let them know!"

CHAPTER THREE

Austin and Alanna climbed down the rigging and raced across the deck, almost crashing into the ship's cook. He was handing out biscuits and drinks to the pirate crew.

Before Austin and Alanna could tell them about the boat, the cook pushed a glass and biscuit into their hands.

"Get this down ye, me hearties. Fill your boots!" said the cook.

"We don't have time for snacks, there are pirates approaching!" Austin cried.

"These aren't bad," Alanna told Austin, her voice muffled by a mouthful of biscuit. "A bit dry, but the raisins are OK."

The cook beamed with pleasure. "That would be the wriggly weevils. They give 'em a nice bit o' crunch and also some chewiness!"

"Euch!" Alanna spat out her biscuit.

"Easy, easy," said the cook, slapping her

back. "You two must be new to the crew. Welcome to the *New Leaf*. That's *New Leaf* by name, *New Leaf* by nature!"

"Mr Cook," Austin said, tapping the cook's arm.

"Stealing treasure's not for us. No sir, not any more!" the cook said, shaking Austin's arm away. "We have a very special map with all the buried treasure on the islands around here marked on it. We're using the map to dig up the treasure and return it to its rightful owners. It's such a good feeling – there's only one thing better than stealing treasure, and that's giving it back!"

"That's great," Alanna said, hopping from foot to foot impatiently. "But we really need to speak to the captain. There is a boat on its wa—"

Alanna was interrupted by Ozzy yapping from inside the barrel where Austin had left him. Austin lifted him out and he ran over to the side of the deck, barking and growling at something over the side of the ship.

Alanna and Austin looked over and saw the pirate's boat was pulling up next to the *New Leaf*.

"Which way are the captain's quarters?" Alanna asked the cook. "It's really important!"

"Hoo, hoo!" Sour Sal, the pirate who'd given them their new names, overheard and bent over double with laughter.

"I'd like to see the mate brave enough to wake our cap'n!" she said.

"But—"

"No buts m'dear, those are the orders! It's impossible to wake the captain up anyhow. Captain sleeps like a stack of logs!"

"But look!" Austin called, a man and a

woman climbed aboard the ship. He noticed
that they had taken off their pirate hats.

"Hullooo! Hullooo!" the new arrivals called.

The woman was tall and the man was short, with a parrot perched on his shoulder.

Before any of the pirates could ask who they were, the tall one bounded over and shook the cook's hand.

"How wonderful to be on the famous *New Leaf* Ship! I'm Bartle." She turned to her companion. "Didn't I say they would be a welcoming crew, Peebee?"

"Welcoming crew! Welcoming crew!" cried the parrot, jumping up and down on the short man's shoulder.

The rest of the *New Leaf* crew gathered around the newcomers.

"We are at your service," said Bartle. "As soon as we heard about the good work you are doing to return stolen treasure to the rightful owners, we came to help!"

Peebee bent down to pet Ozzy. "What a

fine pooch you have there. Here, boy!"

Ozzy growled low in his throat and backed away from the stranger's hand. Peebee stood up, red-faced.

"It's been a long row my friends and our poor arms are tired," said Bartle. "Could we wash the salt off our faces?"

"If yer here to help, then our ship is your ship," said Cook. "You'll find a washing barrel below deck."

The two newcomers said their thanks and then scurried away. Austin noticed them sharing a sly smile with each other as they went. He pulled Alanna aside.

"We should keep an eye on those two," he said. "I've got a bad feeling about them."

"Me too," said Alanna. "And Ozzy doesn't like them either. Let's follow them."

Ozzy barked in agreement.

The twins crept after Peebee and Bartle, being careful to stay out of sight. The inside of the ship was dark and smelt of mouldy apples.

Suddenly, Peebee's parrot squawked loudly.

"Find the map room! Find the map room! Steal the map! Steal the map!"

So that's what they are up to! Austin thought.

"Keep the treasure! Keep the treasure!" screeched the parrot.

Austin shook his head and Alanna narrowed her eyes. The crew of the *New Leaf* were trying to do something good while Peebee and Bartle wanted to steal their precious map and keep all the treasure for themselves.

"We won't let them get away with it!" whispered Alanna.

Austin felt his hands curl into fists. It wasn't fair! "I'll try to distract them while you find the map room."

Alanna nodded and ran down the passageway as fast as she could.

Austin swallowed his fear. The crew of the *New Leaf* were counting on him but now Alanna had gone, he wasn't sure what to do.

"Err, *friends . . .*" he said, trying to keep the tremble out of his voice.

Peebee and Bartle jumped and turned around with a start.

"I've . . . erm . . . I've been sent to invite you to our afternoon show," Austin said, his heart beating fast in his chest.

The two pirates exchanged a glance.

"The *New Leaf* crew have laid on something extra special. You don't want to disappoint them, do you?" asked Austin.

"No, no, of course we don't," Bartle said quickly. "Lead the way, boy!"

Back on the deck, Austin crouched down low beside Ozzy. He lifted Ozzy's velvety ear and whispered in it.

"I think I might have a plan to distract these bad pirates but you've got to help me boy. Follow my lead!"

Ozzy yapped eagerly.

Peebee and Bartle were tapping their feet impatiently and waiting for the show to start. Austin took a deep breath. "Welcome to the

New Leaf ... erm ... dance show!"

Austin busted out his signature dance move called the spin and slide. To his amazement, Ozzy copied him! The dog twirled in a circle as if chasing his tail and then slid to the side. He did understand! Austin kept going. He did the Boggle Wiggle, the Roll-back and Jump, and then the Bum Swish. Ozzy followed him move for move. The crew of the *New Leaf* all gathered round and cheered. Even Peebee

and Bartle seemed mesmerised by the dancing dog! Only their parrot huffed and puffed with impatience.

Before long, the whole crew were singing and dancing. Cook brought out his accordion, adding jaunty music to the fun.

Austin took his chance to slip away while the dancing pirates were swinging Peebee and Bartle around. As he ran back below deck, he checked the watch on his wrist. Almost half the watch face was now shaded in blue. They had to protect the map *and* find the treasure chest before it was too late!

CHAPTER FOUR

"Alanna!" Austin called out, running along the corridor below deck.

"In here, Austin!" Alanna popped her head round a door up ahead and he followed her inside.

In the middle of the room was a HUGE map laid out on an enormous oak table. Austin ran his fingers over the rough parchment, tracing golden outlines of islands, surrounded by blue sea. Alanna pointed at the big red crosses marking treasure spots. They had found the map!

"Quick, let's take it to the cook so Bartle and Peebee can't get their hands on it," said Alanna, carefully rolling up the map.

"Wait," said Austin. "The crew have fallen for those pirates hook, line and sinker. Let's find a hiding place for the map until we can wake the captain up."

"And find the treasure chest! But what if there's not enough time to do both?" asked Alanna, glancing at Austin's watch.

Austin bit his lip. It *was* fun being a pirate, but what if their time ran out and they were stuck here for ever?

Austin hesitated. "The *New Leaf* pirates are trying to do a good thing and I think we should help. If Aunty Kessie were here, she would tell us to follow what's in our heart and I feel like it's the right thing to do – even if we do run out of time."

"Same!" Alanna grinned.

Austin looked around the room for a hiding place and then he noticed a large piece of

parchment in a bin under the desk. Someone had been trying to write sea shanties on it and had scrunched it up and thrown it away.

"Perfect!" Austin rolled up the parchment and grabbed some string from the table to tie it up. Then he swapped the real map for the rolled-up sheet of sea shanties from the bin.

Austin tucked the real map under his arm and headed out of the room.

Alanna followed, but then stopped in her tracks. "I've just had the best idea ever!"

Austin followed her gaze to a bucket of water in the corner, collecting drips from the ceiling. He knew just what his twin was thinking.

"You're a genius!" Austin said, grinning.

They found some more rope and tied it to the bucket. Then, *very carefully*, they stood on a chair and used the door to hoist up the bucket. Austin tied an expert knot to keep it perfectly balanced on top of the slightly open door.

"The next person who pushes this door will get a chilly surprise!" said Alanna, satisfied with their handiwork.

"Let's hope it's Peebee and Bartle!" grinned Austin.

They darted through the belly of the ship, looking for somewhere to hide the real map. In the cook's galley they found a small dusty cupboard filled with brooms and old junk. Perfect! They stashed the map safely out of sight and then raced back onto the deck.

Austin and Alanna found the pirates, exhausted from the dancing and singing, sat down on the floor, passing round drinks and munching heartily on weevil biscuits. Ozzy was still dancing, although he had slowed right down and looked very, *very* tired. Austin

ran over to Ozzy and opened his arms. Ozzy jumped into them, panting from all his effort.

"Well done, boy!" Austin said, ruffling Ozzy's ears.

Bartle and Peebee got up and tried to sneak away on their tip-toes but Alanna and Austin had their eyes on them!

"Where are you going?" Alanna called.

"Who, me?" said Bartle, her hand on her chest as if she could do no wrong.

All the pirates turned to look at them.

"The dancing put me in such a good mood," Bartle said, ignoring Alanna's question. "All I can think about is the wonderful work this crew does. It brings a tear to my eye, it really does."

She patted her pockets and brought out a dirty hankie. She wiped her face, even though it was completely dry.

There were murmurs of appreciation from the crew.

"We would like to add to your wonderful map right now," she continued. "Any treasure we've seen, we'll mark down. I want all those people who've lost their treasure to be reunited with it."

The other pirates cheered.

"Be our guest," said Sour Sal. "The map room is below deck, third door on the right."

Austin clapped his hand to his forehead.

"Don't believe her!" he shouted, but the pirates were already showing Peebee and Bartle below deck.

Austin pointed at his watch. Almost three-quarters of the face had turned to blue. Time was running out!

All of a sudden, the twins heard a loud

CRASH

from below deck, followed by an even louder shriek. Moments later, Peebee and Bartle

came storming back up, soaked from head to foot.

"Looks like your plan worked, Alanna!" Austin whispered.

"Whoever did this to us, I'll throttle 'em with me bare hands!" bellowed Bartle. As she shouted, flecks of water flew from her face and splattered the crew around him.

"First you make us join in your stupid dance and then you drop a bucket of water on us. You rotten pirates don't deserve the treasure!" yelled Peebee.

The crew of the *New Leaf* stared at them open-mouthed. These weren't the friendly, polite pirates they were dancing with just a few minutes ago!

The cook pointed to the rolled-up parchment in Bartle's hand.

"Now hold on one minute, no one gave

you permission to take the map from the map room. That's *our* treasure map, and the treasure belongs to the owners," he said.

Bartle and Peebee looked at one another in panic.

"Quick, scarper!" Peebee cried out to Bartle.

They took off, hurtling across the deck as fast as one pair of tall legs and one pair of short legs could run.

The crew of the *New Leaf* weren't going to let them get away so easily! They sprinted after the thieving pirates, trying to corner them like rats. Peebee and Bartle's parrot flew in circles around the crew, flapping its wings and screeching. It gleefully pooped over as many pirates as it could.

"Wait!" called Alanna. "That's not the real map!"

But the pirates of the *New Leaf* were too busy chasing Peebee and Bartle and didn't hear her over the pounding of their own feet.

Alanna climbed onto a barrel and tried again. "That's not the real map!" she shouted as loudly as she could, but they didn't pay any attention.

Ozzy leapt out of Austin's arms and chased after the culprits too. He sprung onto Peebee's back, who landed with a thump on his tummy. Ozzy bit his trouser leg and growled.

RIIIIIPPP!

Peebee's trousers ripped right off!

"My trousers!" he screeched.

Sour Sal tried to leap over a pail to catch Bartle. She tripped and knocked

it over, spilling a catch of fish across the deck.

BAAANG!

The other pirates slipped over the wet fish, crashing into the sides of the ship.

Bartle and Peebee staggered to their feet, clutching sore elbows and bruised bottoms.

They got to the starboard side, where they had tied up their boat. The two climbed over the edge of the ship and shimmied down the rope.

"We be getting off this stinkin' ship!" Bartle yelled. "But we has the map and soon all the treasure will be ours!"

"All ours! All ours!" their parrot screeched gleefully.

"I really hate that bird," muttered Alanna.

CHAPTER FIVE

Austin looked around at the poor, miserable faces of the *New Leaf's* crew. Most lay on the deck, defeated and bruised. A couple tried to get up, but stumbled, slipped and slid over the wet deck covered in fish, water, feathers and parrot poop.

"The captain will be furious!" wailed Sour Sal. "We've lost our map!"

"But it's not—" Austin began, but the cook drowned him out by starting to sob loudly.

"Our map is gone and our ship's a mess!" he blubbered. "What will the captain say?!"

"What will I say about what?"

All the pirates looked up as Captain Ching stepped onto the deck. Her wild black hair billowed in the wind under her Captain's hat. She stomped across the ship in her big black boots, making the boards of the deck shake. She put her hands on her hips and tutted, looking at the mess that surrounded her.

The cook pointed to the starboard side, too afraid to speak.

Captain Ching leant over the side of her ship, sticking her bottom in the air.

Peebee was rowing away and Bartle was doing a little dance and waving the rolled up parchment, laughing with glee.

Captain Ching turned around, staring at each pirate in turn with her glaring dark eyes.

The cook took off his chef's hat and held it in his hands. He trembled like jelly.

"The treasure map, Captain, is s-s-t-t-t . . ."

". . . stashed safe and sound in the galley!" shouted Austin, jumping in front of the cook.

"Jumpin' Joe and Climbin' Cleo, is this really true?" said Sour Sal.

"Yes! We've been trying to tell you all along!" Alanna grinned and skipped down to the galley to retrieve the map.

"We knew those pirates were up to no good," Austin told the captain. "So we hid the *real* map to keep it safe."

Alanna raced back and handed the rolled-up parchment to Captain Ching.

"We did try and tell you," said Alanna, addressing the New Leaf pirates. "But you wouldn't listen!"

"And," added Austin, "with the send-off we just gave Peebee and Bartle, I don't think you'll be seeing those two for a very long time!"

Captain Ching unrolled the treasure map and the whole crew let out a mighty roar.

"Three cheers for Jumpin' Joe and Climbin' Cleo!" Captain Ching cried.

The crew hoisted the twins and Ozzy onto their shoulders. Austin's face flushed with warmth, they had done it!

"On behalf of my crew and me, I would like

to give you a reward for your bravery and quick thinking. Wait right there, I'll be back in a jiffy." Captain Ching strode off and disappeared below deck.

When the pirates finally put the twins and Ozzy down, Austin checked the painted watch on his wrist.

"Oh no!" he cried, showing the watch face to Alanna. It was almost completely blue. Austin chewed on the inside of his lip. There was no time to go searching for the treasure chest. What would happen to them now their time was up?

Austin took a deep breath. Aunty Kessie and her studio suddenly felt very far away. Alanna put her arm around her brother.

"Maybe it won't be so bad to stay pirates for ever?" she said, although her voice was a bit wobbly.

"We _were_ pretty brave, weren't we?" Austin's voice was a bit wobbly too.

Alanna nodded. "And quick thinking!"

A moment later, Captain Ching returned holding a shiny gold box with delicate engravings. It glittered in the sun.

"This is my own very special treasure chest," she said, beaming from ear to ear. "It was made by my mother, the mighty Captain Chen. And now I am handing it to you, to say thank you for saving our mission."

Austin and Alanna's mouths fell open. It looked just like the treasure chest they were supposed to be looking for!

"THANK YOU! THANK YOU! THANK YOU!" they cried, jumping up and down.

Austin gratefully took the chest. They had done it! They had found the treasure!

He looked at the painted watch on his wrist. The face was now completely blue.

"Quick Alanna, let's try going back the way we came," said Austin. He turned to the crew. "Goodbye *New Leaf* pirates."

"We've had an awesome time, but we have to go now," said Alanna.

They quickly hugged their new friends goodbye. The cook sniffled back some tears.

Austin scooped up Ozzy and held onto him tight. The heavy mist was gathering once again. They ran across the gangplank even though they couldn't see through the mist to the other side.

CHAPTER SIX

Austin and Alanna ran blindly into the grey fog. As they ran, the fog started to clear, and before they knew it, they were standing in Aunty Kessie's back yard once again. The sun was gently setting behind them. There were no blue waves, or seagulls, and there was no sign of the *New Leaf* pirate ship. It was just the three of them with their shadows drawn long across the patio.

Ozzy looked up at the twins and whined.

Alanna gave Austin a quizzical look. "Have we really just been on a pirate ship or did we dream it?"

"We have this," Austin said, holding up the glittering golden casket.

Something green floated down from the sky and landed on Alanna's feet.

"A parrot's feather!" Austin picked it up gently.

The twins grinned at each other. It had all been real!

"Is that you, twin peas?" they heard Aunty Kessie call from the house.

Austin and Alanna looked at each other, their clothes were back to normal but their faces were still painted like pirates. What would

Aunty Kessie think? They ran into the studio with Ozzy behind them, right into Aunty Kessie! She didn't seem surprised by their appearance at all. In fact, she clapped her hands in delight and then wiped Austin's cheek with her thumb.

"I see you've found the face paints," she said with a wink. "Being a pirate suits you both!"

Alanna and Austin shared a glance. Did their aunty know the face paints were *magic*?

"Oh, and you've found my jewellery box too, well done!" said Aunty. She reached out and took the casket. As she turned it in her hands, the box suddenly looked like any old

jewellery box, not a shimmering treasure chest from a pirate at all.

"But Aunty, that's—" said Austin, ready to tell her it was a present from the fearless Captain Ching. Before he could get the words out, Alanna blurted:

"So glad we found it for you, Aunty!"

"What were you saying, Austin, love?" Aunty Kessie asked.

"Oh nothing - nothing at all," mumbled Austin. Maybe it *was* a good idea to keep their adventure to themselves.

Ozzy lay down with his paws over his face. He was going to keep quiet too.

Aunty Kessie tucked the box under her arm. "I was looking all over the house for this. Right, you two twin peas, just fifteen minutes left of painting and then it's time for dinner."

Austin looked at all the different coloured

paints on the table. He suddenly knew exactly what he wanted to draw. He was going to draw the *New Leaf* with all the new friends he had made. And he didn't need to choose what colour to use because he could use them all!

After a short while, Aunty Kessie popped her head around the door.

"Dinner's ready! Make sure you wash your faces before you come to the table."

The twins jumped up, hungry all of a sudden. It had been a long time since the weevil biscuits!

Before they left the studio, Austin couldn't help but take one last look at the face-painting kit. He slowly lifted the lid of the tin. The brush was in its tray, as still as any ordinary brush. Austin turned to Alanna, disappointed, but Alanna pointed at the lid of the tin. There was one last message on the lid:

You've won, well done!
You got the prize.
Come back soon, for faces new,
You won't believe your eyes!

The twins hugged each other in delight. They couldn't wait to try the face paints again soon!

They ran into the kitchen where Aunty was waiting with a warm towel to wipe their faces. She helped them wash their hands and they settled down for dinner.

"Fish soup and fufu, yum," Austin said, his mouth watering. "The perfect end to the perfect day!"

Ozzy took a long drink from his water bowl and then flopped into his dog bed. In no time at all, his eyes closed and he fell asleep. He'd had an exhausting afternoon!

Look out for more MAGIC FACES adventures with Austin and Alanna – coming soon!